T0198830

RINGO RHINO

Tries To Fit In

Josephine C. Force-Rojas

ABOUT THE AUTHOR:

Josephine taught herself to read at the age of four when she felt the pictures in her books weren't satisfying enough, thus leaving her the desire for more details. She then became obsessed with Dr. Seuss' "Green Eggs and Ham" leaving no room for any other books. Josephine is married with three adult children, a step-son, and four beautiful grandchildren. They are her personal supporters and proof-readers, which helps her to reach various audiences. Her hobbies include, writing, drawing, poetry, puzzles, sharing weekly family night with her children, quality family time, vacationing, collecting various paraphernalia, and listening to a diverse genre of music. Her favorite artist is Norman Rockwell. Recreationally, Josephine began writing in the early 1980's although prioritizing her children's education, she stalled although encouraged reading with her children. Though she struggled through multiple trials and tribulations throughout the years, she prevailed. She managed to open an inspiring blog in 2015, fell ill and she drifted. Late 2016 she opened her home to her mother following her first shoulder surgery, in order to tend to her mother's Dementia dilemma for a year and a half; until her mother's unfortunate passing in March 2018. In 2019, Josephine decided to restart where she had left off by reaching the minds and hearts of all people through her natural stature and writing, always adding a little rhyme in her style for a little pizazz and fun!

ABOUT THE ILLUSTRATOR

Faith Marie Force is a young determined artist of various mediums. She graduated high school in 2017 where she took a Digital Art Class using the Adobe Illustrator program including numerous other programs. Currently she's utilizing the ArtRage 5 program. She familiarized herself with an array of paintings using different techniques which she has done professional work. She has two and a half years' experience in the workforce teaching art classes. Faith has produced outstanding artwork pieces by using watercolors, colored pencils, acrylics, and oil bases, as well as multiple paint markers of different substances. Faith even sketched her own self-portrait, a mural, and multiple mystic pieces. She is currently maintaining a multiple work employment career of four jobs! She's a child 's book illustrator in the morning, an assistant teacher at a local pre-school in the afternoon, an art teacher several nights a week, as well as a part time baby sitter. She is an exceptionable inspiring young lady with wonderful opportunities ahead of her. I for one am proud that she is the illustrator for my first published book! Sincerely, Josephine C. Force- Rojas

AuthorHouse™
1663 Liberty Drive
Bloomington, IN 47403
www.authorhouse.com
Phone: 1 (800) 839-8640

Because of the dynamic nature of the Internet, any web addresses or links contained in
this book may have changed since publication and may no longer be valid. The views
expressed in this work are solely those of the author and do not necessarily reflect the
views of the publisher, and the publisher hereby disclaims any responsibility for them.

Any people depicted in stock imagery provided by Getty Images are models,
and such images are being used for illustrative purposes only.
Certain stock imagery © Getty Images.

This book is printed on acid-free paper.

ISBN: 978-1-7283-3521-6 (sc)
ISBN: 978-1-7283-3523-0 (hc)
ISBN: 978-1-7283-3522-3 (e)

Print information available on the last page.

Published by AuthorHouse 11/12/2019

authorHOUSE®

RINGO RHINO

TRIES TO FIT IN

MY DEDICATION:

Dedicated to my belated Mother, Olive May Josephine

Special Thanks and Love to GOD, My Husband: Rodolfo, My Children: Sebastian, Marilyn May, and Jonathan Adam, My grandchildren: Rory Leilani, Colton Xavier AKA-'Cole', Raymond Eugene Snyder V AKA-'Quintin', & Laural May Josephine AKA-'JoJo'

Ringo Rhino is a friendly rhino. He just wants to fit in. No matter how hard he tries, everywhere he goes, trouble begins. Ringo woke up to the morning sun as he usually does. He loves to sing and dance with everyone!

He started his day brushing his teeth, when the toothpaste squished under his feet. He wasn't sad, instead he was glad because today he was going wear his beautiful plaid.

"*Today will be different from all other days, for this is the day I will ask Miss Dixie to be my friend,*" Ringo said as his day began.

As he started his day heading his way, he thought he just might, look for a gift that was just right. He stopped by a store but had trouble with the door.

It wasn't long after he went in, did trouble soon begin. He ran into Lioness Leilani and said to her instead, *"Good day Mr. Lion, I hope everything is all right."* She became offended. Clearly, **SHE** was not a **HE**.

She held back from saying anything mean with all her might. *"Clearly you are mistaken Rhino-Bite!"* Then she snubbed her snout with a little clout and went on her way. Ringo decided this wasn't the perfect place.

Ringo walked down the street to see others he might want to meet. He stopped at a stand because he heard a musical band.

As he followed the sounds that vibrated the grounds, he begun to hum. Then for some silly reason, he snatched a guitar and begun to strum. Then he threw it down onto the ground, then picked up a drum and begun to bung!

The Musical Band did not understand then yelled at Ringo, *"Go mingo at some other stand,"* scolded the band.

Ringo was only trying to blend, with anyone that would be his friend.

That's when he stumbled upon a small duck pond. When there in the midst, he heard something *HSSS! HSSS!* Up popped a snake making him shake.

"Hello there, my name is Jake and I am a snake, would you like to share a piece of cake?" Ringo was surprised as he looked into his gazing eyes and realized he'd better keep going by. "No, thank you," he replied.

With fear on his face, Ringo picked up the pace. Then he tripped over a stick in the grass that was thick.

"I don't know how but this must be a silly trick!"

At that moment Jake the Snake decided to strike! Ringo yelled out a spell, **"OUCH!"** as he looked at his leg on the right and that nasty bite! *"Why would you strike at someone who's nice?"* Ringo asked without a fight.

"I did it out of spite!" Exclaimed Jake the Snake. "You see, I've never been able to make others like me. I have no friends you see? So, I give no breaks, instead I take, and to me you look like a juicy steak!" said Jake the Snake.

"How about, **I** be your friend and we can put that to an end? If you promise never to bite me again," offered Ringo.

Jake agreed to Ringo's offer and handed
him a toy flying saucer.

They said over tea, *"Friends we shall be!"* Ringo started to say, *"I have been thinking all day long for some kind of way to make Miss Dixie aware that I care."*

That's when you came along as a friend I have longed.
Now I feel like I belong. Thank you, Jake. Till now, I never
met a friendly snake."

That's when, to himself Ringo thought, *"I think I aught, though it may be a long shot. I can use this toy, and with just a little coy…YES! I shall send a note and fly it over Miss Dixie's head with a message I've wrote."*

"I will tie a small note with a ribbon of pink, to the end of this, I think. The note will say, **"I like you Miss Dixie and want you to be my friend someday."**

Miss Dixie saw the note that Ringo wrote. She especially loved the color he chose of course. She said, *"I like you too, Ringo Rhino."*

"Will you join me at the Disco Diner? You see, I like you best from all the rest, because you have zest!"

From that moment on, Ringo was proud and honored, to finally feel he belonged.

The three of them were friends that lasted long.

He called it a win, because all he ever wanted, was to fit in!

THE END

GLOSSARY

Aught: Anything at all; Should.

Belonged: To be part of a group or organization; member.

Bung: To hit or bang with hands, like on an instrument.

Clout: Influence like with power; Expression of authority.

Coy: Holding back details; not saying what they wish to say.

Gaze: Look with surprise, like with a stare.

Nasty: Unpleasant to sight or smell; Unpleasant harmful person or thing.

Plaid: Checkered cloth or shirt usually made of wool.

Snatch: To grab quickly.

Snout: Nose and/or mouth of an animal.

Snub: To ignore; pretend not to notice.

Spite: To offend or annoy; choose to bother.

Squish: To push pressure on sometimes making noise; squash.

Strike: To purposely hit to cause damage; Hit with weapon.

Strum: To play an instrument like a guitar by using fingers or a pick.

Vibrate: A low rumble movement made from music, engines, volcanoes, etc.

Zest: One showing enthusiasm and energy.

Printed in the United States
By Bookmasters